KILLER IN
THE WOODS

David G. Tapp

ISBN- 1720530130
ISBN- 9781720530138

DEDICATION

I want to thank the Lord for allowing me to have the love and support of my family and friends.

I also want to thank my friends and co-workers, Brian and Lance. You guys were a big help. Thanks! Thank you, Lisa, for taking time to read my manuscript.

CHAPTER 1

Willow Springs, Texas
1980

It was a crisp, clear night in the small East Texas town of Willow Springs. The kind of night where the deer like to go foraging for food under the starry skies. A twelve-point buck was eating his share of acorns underneath the oak trees that were located next to farmer Frank Tincher's property. The huge buck luckily managed to elude the hunters again this season. Even though deer season was over, given the opportunity, some hunters would be willing to break the law, just so they could kill the big buck. Maybe not for the meat, but for the antlers and the bragging rights. Hunting at night is illegal, but to brothers Craig and John Shannon, the towns hooligans, spot-lighting for deer and hogs was an adventure. They had no respect for the sport of hunting and little for the law. As they drove slowly down County Road 16 with their spot-light shining into the pastures on both sides of the road something large caught John's attention.

"Craig stop the truck!" he said in excitement.

"What is it John?" Craig asked.

"I thought I seen something moving just on the other side of the fence."

Craig parked his old Ford pickup on the side of the road.

"Kill the motor." insisted John.

While they sat quietly, the large twelve-point buck jumped the fence into Mr. Tincher's pasture.

"Did you see it?" whispered John.

"Yeah, I did. Looks like that big buck every one's been trying to get. Grab your gun, I'll carry the flashlight."

"I don't think that's a good idea." warned John. "That buck just jumped into Mr. Tincher's property. You know he don't like people on his land, much less people trespassing."

"Don't be scared. That old man is probably asleep. He won't even know we're here."

Slowly they made their way across the ditch and stood next to an old barbed wire fence.

Craig exhaled and blew steam from his mouth.

"Let's make this quick. It's cold out here. I should have worn my big coat."

John was the first to crawl through the fence.

"Give me the gun."

After handing John the gun, Craig was able to get through the loose fence without snagging his clothes on the barbs.

"It's a good thing Mr. Tincher isn't on top of his fence mending." whispered Craig.

Shining their flashlight in front of them, they kept an eye out for the large buck. After walking a hundred yards, they stopped.

"That big boy got to be around here somewhere."

muttered Craig. John aimed the light beam at the fence row where a cluster of oak trees stood.

"Hey, look! There he is. Aim in on him."

Craig looked through his scope. Feeling confident in his aim, he fired off a round. The bullet penetrated a tree, missing the buck by a few inches.

The buck jumped the fence and then took off running.

"Dadgumitt!" yelled Craig. "I think I got him."

"Come on." suggested John. Let's go see if we can find a blood trail."

The sound from the rifle woke Mr. Tincher.

"Sounds like I got some visitors." he said to himself. "Well let's see what ole Killer has to say about that." After getting dressed, Mr. Tincher grabbed his rifle and went outside and stood on his back porch. He could easily look down-hill and see the light from the flashlight move across his pasture. Mr. Tincher leaned his gun against the back-porch wall, then proceeded on to the barn. After he entered the barn, Mr. Tincher said, "Killer, you've got some work to do." Inside a steel cage was a six-hundred-pound hog. His tusks were every bit of six inches long. Great for tearing open the flesh of creatures, even humans. Mr. Tincher raised him from a small piglet, training him to protect his property from all unwanted visitors.

As soon as Mr. Tincher opened the cage door, he yelled, "Sick'em boy!"

The large beast ran out of his cage like a thoroughbred running from the starting gates at the Kentucky Derby. After he released the beast, Mr. Tincher went back to his back porch to retrieve his rifle. It was in a matter of seconds before the hog had reached its prey. Killer had caught Craig and John off guard. Craig was the first to be attacked. With his huge size and quick speed, Killer knocked Craig to the ground causing him to drop his gun and to lose his breath. Slashing his sharp tusks into Craig's stomach, the blood-crazed hog began to maul him. Screaming in agony, it didn't take Craig long to expire. John stood in shock. Knowing that his brother was dead, he turned and started to run for dear life. Seeing the light from the flashlight leaving the scene, Mr. Tincher aimed in on John.

He smirked, "Where do you think you're going?" He pulled the trigger. A second later, the flashlight hit the ground. The bullet entered the back of John's head, killing him instantly.

Knowing he had two bodies to bury now, Mr. Tincher placed a coach's whistle in his mouth and gave two short blows. Hearing the sound of the whistle, Killer knew it was time for him to return to his cage. Once he was secured back in his cage, Mr. Tincher used a water hose to rinse the blood off of Killers head.

"Good job, Killer!" he chuckled.

After rinsing the hog clean, Mr. Tincher, dumped a dozen ears of corn into the cage.

"Here you go boy, in case you didn't get enough to eat."

Mr. Tincher then pick up a shovel and started on his way to bury the two Shannon boys.

CHAPTER 2

Early the next morning, Lt. Chris Finch of the Willow Springs Police Department, was sitting at his desk getting his day started with the help of a cup of fresh brewed coffee. His phone rang.

"Police department, Lt Finch speaking."

"Finch, Tincher here. I need you to come by my house as soon as you can."

Lt. Finch cupped his hand over his mouth trying to conceal his conversation.

"I told you not to be calling me here. What do you want?" he whispered.

"You need to come see me!" insisted Mr. Tincher.

"Alright, I'll be out there. I got some things I need to do first."

"Ok. But make it snappy."

As he left his office, Lt. Finch met Police Chief Tom McKechnie entering the police station.

"Good morning Chief."

"Hey, good morning Finch. Where are you heading out to?"

"Sir, I thought I'd make some rounds this morning while I'm caught up on my paper work."

Chief McKechnie laughed, "Yeah right. You're going to make a round through the drive-thru at the donut shop."

Lt. Finch grinned, "Sir, you know me too well."

"Since you're going that way, pick me up some too, while you're at it. The Misses wasn't up to cooking this morning."

"Ok, I got you covered." replied Lt. Finch.

With his mind wondering on why Mr. Tincher was so impatient in wanting to see him, Lt. Finch quickly drove passed the donut shop not even giving it a single thought.

CHAPTER 3

After traveling five miles out of town, he turned off the main highway onto County Road 16. Even as a child, Lt. Finch always got an eerie feeling when he traveled down the long-secluded road. The tall trees made a canopy over the road, making it look as if you were traveling through a large dark tunnel. It was spooky especially at night. Lt. Finch always wondered what he would do if some scary creature jumps down from the trees and landed on the hood of his car. Would he speed up then slow down trying to sling off the uninvited passenger, or would he simply pull out his weapon and shoot through the windshield. The thought still made him shiver. At that moment he was happy it was daylight out. After passing through the tunnel of trees, Lt. Finch slowed down so he could inspect the old Ford pickup that was parked beside the road. Slowly passing by, he knew it belonged to the Shannon boys. He said to himself, "What are you boys up to? I'm sure it's no good."

Looking to his left, Lt. Finch could see in the

distance Mr. Tincher's house. It sat on top of a hill, which overlooked two hundred acres of land.

As he approached the entrance to Mr. Tincher's property, Lt. Finch turned off of the county road, and slowly drove up the long and winding driveway. He parked his squad car in front of Mr. Tincher's house. Out of common courtesy, he honked his horn. Mr. Tincher opened his front door and stepped out onto his porch. He then asked, "Does anyone know you came out here?"

"No." answered Lt. Finch. "Why the secrecy?"

"Has anyone been looking for those Shannon boys yet?"

"I haven't heard anything this morning. I did see their pickup. It's parked down the road close to your property line."

Mr. Tincher handed Lt. Finch two wallets. Looking through the first wallet, he pulled out a driver's license. It belonged to Craig Shannon. He then searched through the second wallet and found the license for John Shannon.

"Where did you get these?" asked Lt. Finch.

"From them."

"Did you have a confrontation with them?"

"No."

"So, you're telling me you just walked up to them and they handed over their wallets?"

"I took the wallets from their bodies."

Lt. Finch pulled his shades off.

"What did you do?"

"I heard a gunshot last night. I went outside on my porch and I saw a light flashing around in my pasture. I don't like people snooping around on my property. You know I've got our business to protect."

"What did you do then?" questioned Lt. Finch.

"I turned Killer loose on them."

"I guess he killed both of them, huh?"

"No, he didn't. While he was taking care of one, the other tried to run away, but I shot him before he could escape."

"What did you do with the bodies?"

"I buried them."

"Hope you buried them deep. We don't want the smell to draw attention around here. Is there anything else you need to tell me?"

"I need you to help me hide their pickup. I can pull it with my tractor if you will steer. We can store it in my barn."

Lt. Finch asked, "Why didn't you drive it up here?"

"I couldn't find the keys." grumbled Mr. Tincher.

"Did you check their pockets?"

"Yes, I did. I'm thinking the one that Killer got a hold of must have had them. His clothes were shredded to pieces. They're lost out there somewhere."

"Ok, let's hurry. Chief McKechnie is waiting for his donuts."

CHAPTER 4

With the killing of the Shannon brothers weighing heavily on his mind, Lt. Finch returned back to the police station, forgetting to stop by the donut shop. As he opened the door to his office, Chief McKechnie yelled out to him.

"Finch! Where's my donuts?"

He walked over to the Chief's office and stood in the doorway.

"Sorry sir, I forgot. I got tied up helping an old man get his stalled pickup off the side of the road. It completely slipped my mind."

"That's Ok. You helping someone out of a jam is more important. Oh, before you go, have you seen the Shannon brothers driving around in that old Ford truck of theirs?"

Feeling antsy, Lt. Finch said, "No. What makes you ask that?"

The Chief leaned back in his chair, causing it to make a loud squeaking sound, "Mrs. Shannon said her two boys were out last night and they never returned back home. She said it wasn't like them being gone this long. I told her I would give them twenty-four hours before we put out an APB for her missing boy's."

"I wouldn't worry about them two. They're probably parked on some back road trying to sober up before they go home." Lt. Finch suggested.

"Yeah, you're probably right. Those two boys get themselves into more trouble. I really don't see them living to be old men. They're going to come across the wrong person one day." he warned.

"You're right about that." Lt. Finch said as he walked back to his office. After closing his door, he said, *"Chief you don't know how right you are."*

CHAPTER 5

The next morning, Lt. Finch, and his wife Sara were sitting at the kitchen table, having breakfast and reading the newspaper. While letting her coffee cool down she said, "Honey, Mrs. Shannon called while you were in the shower. She said her boys have been missing, going on two days now." She sounded upset. She asked me if I would keep a look out for them."

Lt. Finch got up from the table and placed his plate in the sink.

"She reported them missing yesterday. Chief McKechnie said he would file a missing person's report after the twenty-four-hour grace period. We'll start hanging up missing person posters around town and in the surrounding communities."

"That poor lady. I can't imagine what she's going through." she lamented.

Lt. Finch grabbed the keys to his new Chevy Camaro from the kitchen counter.

Sara laid the newspaper down.

"It's your day off, where're you going this morning

in such a hurry?"

Trying to think of something fast. He opens the front door. "Ah, I'm going to take the car for a spin. It needs to be washed too. I won't be gone too long. Love you."

Closing the door behind him, he quickly trotted off to the car. Starting up the eight-cylinder engine, Lt. Finch revved it up. He loved the sound that the powerful engine made. After backing out from the garage, he peeled out of the driveway onto the street. While on his way to visit with Mr. Tincher, his drug trafficking partner, Lt. Finch made a quick stop at Sally's Flower Shop, one of his main marijuana distribution sites.

Once he finally arrived at Mr. Tincher's house, Lt. Finch honked his horn. After waiting a few minutes, he decided to go look for him. As he walked around the side of the house, Lt. Finch met Mr. Tincher holding a rifle. "It's me! Don't shoot!"

Mr. Tincher lowered his rifle and aimed it at the ground. "Sorry, I didn't recognize the car. You know how leery of strangers I am."

"I just bought the car a week ago. How do you like it?"

"She's pretty. A little flashy for a police officer to be driving, don't you think?"

"I bought it for my wife, Sara."

"Hope Chief McKechnie don't start asking you a lot of questions on how you can afford to buy it."

"Don't worry. I don't drive it around too much. And on top of that, it's no one's business how I spend my money."

"What brings you out here this morning?" Mr. Tincher asked.

"I stopped by Sally's Flower Shop this morning and Jim Session, the owner, ordered five pounds of Willow Springs finest."

"Ok, let's get in my truck and we'll go down to the greenhouses and see if we have some ready."

While driving in the pasture, they pass by a herd of cattle eating hay. "Mr. Tincher, your cattle are fat."

"Thanks. I keep them well fed. That's how I hide some of my money. Some people wash their money through legitimate business. I buy and sale cattle. You have to show some kind of expenditures, as not to be too suspicious."

"Aw, I see." replied Lt. Finch.

In the middle of a thicket of woods, Mr. Tincher had cleared out a two-acre spot where he had twelve large greenhouses built. In each greenhouse was the best marijuana plants East Texas had to offer. Not only did he have a large pond for his cattle to drink, but he had an irrigation line that ran from the pond to each greenhouse to keep his plants watered. The cold weather was no problem either. Each greenhouse had its own diesel-powered generator to keep the growing lights on. Once they had reached the inner sanctum of the woods, Mr. Tincher parked beside a white Toyota pickup.

"Who's here?" Lt. Finch asked.

"That's my nephew Ross Godwin. He's been helping me out on the farm for the past few weeks." Lt. Finch felt concerned.

"Can we trust him to keep his mouth shut about our operation?"

"Oh yeah. He's not a youngster. Ross is twenty-five years old. He has a wife and two kids he has to support. I'm paying him more than he's ever made before. I also made it clear, I hate snitches."

"Good, I'd like to meet him."

Once they entered into the greenhouse that they had parked beside, Lt. Finch smiled when he seen the long rows of tall bushy marijuana plants. With the high humidity in the climate-controlled greenhouse, he felt as though he was walking through the jungles in South American.

Mr. Tincher yelled out, "Ross! Where are you?"

Ross stood up from the table where he was bagging up the marijuana. He waved his arms.

"I'm here in the back, Uncle Frank!"

"Follow me Finch. Let's see what he's doing."

They slowly lumbered their way through the forest of marijuana plants, having to brush aside the leaves from hitting them in the face. As they came to the end of the row, they met up with Ross.

"Hey Ross, this is Lt. Finch of the Willow Springs Police Department."

Ross' eyes opened wide. He started to stutter and shake as he stuck out his hand to greet Lt. Finch.

"Don't worry Ross. He's in business with me." explained Mr. Tincher.

Ross felt a sigh of relief.

"I'm out on parole. If I get busted again, I'll get twenty to life next time."

"If you keep this to yourself, you won't have to worry about that, will you?" warned Lt. Finch

"Yes sir, my mouth is sealed."

"Well good. I have a customer that needs five pounds of Willow Spring. Do you have any ready?"

"Yes sir, I just weighed and bagged some up."

"Good! I'll take it."

After picking up his order, Lt. Finch looked at the

rows of marijuana. He smiled and cheered, "Wow! Keep up the good work guys. Look at all of that money we're going to make."

CHAPTER 6

In past practices, when Lt. Finch would enter into Sally's Flower Shop, he would always case the place out, making sure there weren't any customers around. It would look too suspicious of him entering the shop carrying a black plastic unmarked bag. After walking around the shop and not finding a single customer, Lt. Finch walked to his car to retrieve the merchandise.

Carrying the bag tucked inside his jacket, he saw one of his patrolmen entering the parking lot. He waved and continued in. Not wasting any time, he ran to the back of the shop and handed the bag to Mr. Sessions.

"Here, hide this! One of my men is in the parking lot. It's Officer Coats, with our drug sniffing dog, Buddy. I swear that darn dog can smell drugs a mile away."

"Oh crap!"

Jim grabbed the bag of weed and placed it inside his safe. After securing the door, he felt somewhat at ease.

"Relax Jim. Just calm down. I'll go see what he wants."

Lt. Finch slowly peeped around the corner of the office. Not seeing anyone walking around. He looked back at Jim.

"I don't see anyone. He's probably waiting for me outside."

Jim handed Lt. Finch an envelope full of cash.

"It better all be here." warned Lt. Finch. "We don't want to upset my supplier. If you need more, let me know. I'll be making my rounds."

As he walked out the front door, he saw Officer Coats standing next to his car checking it out.

"That's a real nice ride you got there, Lieutenant."

"Thanks, Coats. Just don't let that dog out. He might pee on my wheels."

They both laughed.

Buddy started barking, then he started sniffing the air.

"Calm down boy. It's only Lt. Finch."

Feeling uneasy that Buddy may have picked up a scent, Lt. Finch quickly got into his car.

"Hey Coats, I have to go. I've got to run some errands before I go home. I'll see you later."

"Take your time lieutenant. I don't want to pull you over for speeding." joked Officer Coats.

"Gee thanks." Lt Finch said with a smirk on his face. By the end of the day, Lt. Finch had visited Leo's One Stop and several residences in Willow Springs that help distribute his product.

CHAPTER 7

Four-thirty that afternoon, Game Warden Jess Jackson entered the lobby of The Willow Springs Police Department.

"Good afternoon sir, can I help you?"

He looked around and saw a red headed woman retrieving a soft drink from a vending machine.

"Yes ma'am. I'm Game Warden Jess Jackson. I hope I'm not too late. I wanted to talk to the chief of police."

She walked up and introduced herself.

"Good afternoon, I'm Kim Speaker, Chief McKechnie's secretary. Let me see if he's free at the moment."

Ms. Speaker walked to Chief McKechnie's office. Seeing that his door was open, she gently tapped on it and said, "Sir, Game Warden Jackson is here. He said he would like to speak with you."

"Sure, send him on in."

Ms. Speaker looked back at Mr. Jackson and beckoned him to come to Chief McKechnie's office.

As he approached Ms. Speaker, he smiled and tipped his hat, "Thanks ma'am."

Chief McKechnie got up from his desk and met Mr. Jackson at the door. He extended out his hand.

"Good afternoon sir. I'm Chief McKechnie."

"Hello Chief, I'm Game Warden Jess Jackson. It's a pleasure to meet you."

Chief McKechnie pointed to a chair in front of his desk.

"Please have a seat. Take a load off."

"Thank you, sir."

While Chief McKechnie walked around his desk to sit down, he asked, "What brings you here, if you don't mind me asking?"

Mr. Jackson pulled off his cowboy hat and placed it on his lap.

"Chief, I'm new in this county and I wanted to spend some time getting to meet the law enforcement personnel in the county. We might need each other's help one day."

"Welcome Mr. Jackson, that sounds good. We worked well with the previous Game Warden, Mr. Mettier. I hope he's enjoying the retirement life."

"I heard he was really good at his job. I hope I can attain his stature."

"Just be careful out there." warned Chief McKechnie. "Working alone can be dangerous."

Mr. Jackson saw a missing persons flyer on the Chief's desk. He picked it up.

"You mind if I take a look?"

"No, go ahead. We just got them in today. We are dispersing them out now. The Shannon brothers have been missing for two days now. They're notorious for spotlighting and hunting at night. The night of their disappearance, an old farmer, Mr. Tincher, called us saying he had seen someone spotlighting along County Road 16 that night. I sent Lt. Finch out to investigate, and he couldn't find anything."

"He didn't find any spent shell casings or even tire tracks?" Mr. Jackson inquired. Standing outside the door ease dropping on their conversation, Lt. Finch cut in and spoke up. "That would be hard finding tracks on an asphalt road." Sounding surprised, "Hey Finch, what are you doing up here on your day off?" asked Chief McKechnie.

Trying to think of an excuse, "I was target practicing and I ran out of bullets. I came up here to get a box."

"Hey Finch, I want you to meet Jess Jackson. He's the new Game Warden."

Lt. Finch and Mr. Jackson shook hands.

"Lt. Finch, Chief said you didn't find any evidence what so ever."

"I looked around. I didn't even see any foot prints."

"If you don't mind, I'd like to take a look myself. I may wait until tonight just to see if I can catch someone out spotlighting. How do I get to County Road 16?"

Take Main Street out to the red light. Turn right and head east for five miles, and County Road 16 will be on the right." explained Chief McKechnie.

After shaking hands, Mr. Jackson left Chief McKechnie's office like a man on a mission. Chief McKechnie turned to Lt. Finch, "The youngster seems to be really motivated. These hunters and fisherman better be on the up and up."

"I'll see you later Chief. I need to go."

"Aren't you forgetting something?" Chief McKechnie asked.

"I don't think so."

"You came in to get a box of ammo for target practice."

"Oh yeah. I'll get them some other time. Something has come up that I need to attend to."

Lt. Finch got into his car and hastily departed. Not wanting to waste any time, he sped out to Mr. Tincher's farm to give him the heads up on the new and energetic Game Warden.

CHAPTER 8

Once Lt. Finch reached Mr. Tincher's house, he gave a short burst on the horn.

Mr. Tincher walked out of his house chewing on a fried chicken leg.

"Sorry for interrupting your meal, but you need to be on the lookout. I just met the new Game Warden. He's young, ambitious and already asking questions about the disappearance of the Shannon boys."

Mr. Tincher placed the half-eaten chicken leg in the front bib pocket of his overalls.

He snickered, "I'll save it for Killer. He likes a little meat left on the bone. So, you say we got us a new Game Warden, huh?"

"I just met him back at headquarters." replied Lt. Finch.

Mr. Tincher grabbed a tooth pick that was laying on his ear. He started picking his teeth and spitting pieces of chicken to the ground.

"Well, I'll put it this way. He won't have any trouble with me, as long as he stays away.

But if he goes to snoopin' around here, his career will be a short one."

"While I'm here, I need a pound of Willow. I'm playing poker with some friends tonight. One of them is a good customer of ours."

"Yeah, hold on. I have some already bagged up in the kitchen."

As Mr. Tincher started walking towards his house, Lt. Finch asked, "Hey, I'm low on money right now. Can you spot me five hundred dollars for tonight?"

"Sure."

After a few minutes of waiting, Mr. Tincher came back with a black plastic bag containing the pound of weed. He then reached into his pocket and pulled out a large sum of cash. He counted out five one hundred-dollar bills.

"Here you go. Good luck tonight and thanks for the information."

CHAPTER 9

One o'clock in the morning, on his way home from Cody Johnson's house, Lt. Finch didn't know if it was the drinking or losing the five hundred-dollars that made his head spin. As he approached County Road 16, he saw Game Warden Jackson turn onto the county road.

He thought to himself, *'Boy you don't know what your fixing to get yourself into. You better quit while you can.'*

After driving down the county road for a half mile, Mr. Jackson decided to park on the side of the road underneath the thick canopy of trees. He turned off the engine and headlights. The only sound made was coming from the occasional traffic on his two-way radio. After sitting still for thirty minutes, he had no luck in hearing the sound of a single gunshot in the distance or a flashlight shining aimlessly on the side of the road. Mr. Jackson became antsy, so he started up his truck and continued further down the darkened path.

After driving far enough to clear the tunnel of

trees, he pulled over and stopped again. Bored, Mr. Jackson stepped out of his pickup and lit up a cigarette. Looking around while he took a drag off his cigarette, he saw a faint light in the woods. Eager to investigate, he took one last puff, before discarding his cigarette to the ground. Carefully making his way down to the fence line, Mr. Jackson kept his flashlight facing the ground searching for fresh tracks. Before he attempted to climb through the barbed wire fence, he found a set of car keys on the ground, partially covered in mud. After wiping the mud from the key chain, Mr. Jackson could see the name Shannon engraved on it. After inspecting it, he placed the keys in his coat pocket. On his second attempt, he was able to climb through the fence without snagging his uniform. Wanting to conceal himself, he carefully walked through the pasture using only the light from starry night sky. He stopped for a moment to see if he could hear anything. Mr. Jackson heard the faint sound of a motor running. As he continued on, the closer to the woods he got, the louder and more distinctive it became.

When he arrived at the edge of the woods, he saw where the light was coming from. It was coming from a flashlight Ross was using when he was checking the fuel levels in the generators. After checking on the last generator, Ross began to mosey his way back to the front of the greenhouse. Before he made his way back, he saw someone walking down towards him. Knowing it wasn't Mr. Tincher, he turned his flashlight off and ran into the woods to hide. After searching the area for the individual he saw walking around, Mr. Jackson was curious to find out why would someone be working this late at night.

He opened the door to one of the greenhouse's. With the help from the growing lamps, he could clearly see hundreds of mature marijuana plants. While he was busy inspecting the other greenhouse's, Ross managed to run up to Mr. Tincher's house undetected. He knocked on Mr. Tincher's back door and yelled, "Uncle Frank!"

Moments later, Mr. Tincher answered the door while pulling up his overalls, "What's going on Ross?" Trying to catching his breath he said, "Someone is searching through the greenhouses!"

"Who is it?"

"I don't know. I took off running."

"Well. we'll see what Killer has to say about it."

Before Mr. Jackson inspected the last greenhouse, he noticed a horrible odor emanating from it. Once he opened the door, the smell made him gag. With no growing lights on, he had to use his flashlight. With his flashlight in his left hand, he knew to keep his shooting hand free in case he had to draw down on someone. But in order to investigate further, he had to cover his nose from the stench with a handkerchief using his right hand. As he made his way through the greenhouse, he saw nothing but tools and bags of fertilizers. He knew some fertilizers didn't smell like rose's, but they didn't smell like death neither. Reaching the back of the greenhouse, he found two separate mounds of dirt. Mr. Jackson found a shovel nearby. Laying his flashlight on the ground, he started scooping away the top layer of dirt on the first mound. After digging through one foot of earth, he found what he figured was the decaying body of one of the Shannon brothers. Before he could start excavating the other shallow grave, Mr. Jackson had to step outside to get some fresh air. Seeing the light flickering in the woods, Mr. Tincher knew he had an intruder. He knew if it was the new Game Warden, back-up would be coming soon. Wasting no time, Mr. Tincher scurried off to the barn to unleashed the six hundred pounds of nightmare on the poor soul who wasn't welcomed. "Sick'em boy!"

As Killer made his way to the unsuspecting Game Warden, Mr. Tincher got into his pickup, and slowly followed him. After catching his breath from the foul odor, Mr. Jackson grabbed his two-way radio from his duty belt in order to call for back-up. Before he could make the call, Mr. Jackson heard the thundering sound of stomping hoofs. He grabbed his side arm and pointed his flashlight indiscriminately, trying to see where the noise was coming from. Killer was on top of him before he knew it. Mr. Jackson was hit with such force from the massive hog, that he crashed through the greenhouse. Not able to defend himself now, Killer did what he was good at. He started to maul the new energetic Game Warden to death. When the screaming in agony had stopped, Mr. Tincher pulled out his trusty whistle and gave it two short bursts. Within a few seconds, Killer stopped the feeding frenzy and then trotted his way back to the barn. "Good boy." commented Mr. Tincher as killer passed by. After securing Killer in his cage, Mr. Tincher drove back down to the greenhouse in order to dig his third grave.

CHAPTER 10

After a night of drinking and gambling, ten o'clock in the morning came too soon for Lt. Finch. He rolled over and noticed his wife was gone.

"I bet she's upset with me." he said to himself. Lt. Finch got up and walked to the kitchen and poured himself a cup of coffee. He read a note she left by the coffee maker.

"Gone to church. Be back soon, you heathen."

Lt. Finch knew he had an hour before she came back home. He decided to call Mr. Tincher, to see if he had any dealings with the Game Warden last night. As the phone was ringing, Lt. Finch knew not to mention any names on the phone because he knew all phone calls could be recorded.

"Hello. This is Frank Tincher."

"Mr. Tincher, Finch here. Have any visitors last night?"

"I sure did. I hope Killer took care of him before the Calvary was notified. He could have exposed everything."

"If he hadn't, your place would have been covered

up with them. How about the vehicle?"

"*It was taken care of.*"

"There's going to be people out searching for him. I'll do my best to steer them away from you. If someone wants to talk to you, play dumb."

"*Ok. I can do that. By the way, how did the poker game go last night?*"

"I didn't do so well. Lost all of my money and gained a hangover from Hades."

Mr. Tincher laughed, "You're not as young as you used to be. You should know your limit. At least you made it home last night, I know of one person that didn't."

CHAPTER 11

Two days had passed since the demise of Game Warden Jackson. Lt. Finch new the heat would be coming down soon in the small town. He was right. While sitting in Chief McKechnie's office talking about last night's boxing match, the telephone rang.

"Good morning. Chief McKechnie speaking."

"Chief McKechnie, I'm Major Ken Young, Region Three Game Warden's supervisor. I need to know if you or any of your officers may have seen Game Warden, Jackson?"

"Yes sir, we have. Mr. Jackson stopped by the station two days ago. He said he wanted to introduce himself since he was new in the county."

"I'm a little concerned. He hasn't check in with me in the last twenty-four hours. In his last transmission, he mentioned that he was going to stake out County Road 16. He said you had a real problem with spotlighting and poachers."

"Yeah, he's referring to the Shannon brothers. They've been reported missing. I explained to him I had sent out my most experienced officer to investigate and he didn't find anything. Mr. Jackson seemed very adamant in checking it out for himself."

"I'll see if the sheriff can send some deputies in to help with the search. Hopefully the Texas Rangers will give us a hand. Any help you can give, will be greatly appreciated."

"Get all the help you can, we'll be glad to assist you." Chief McKechnie replied.

After hanging the phone up he looked at Lt. Finch.

"It's fixing to get busy around here, as you just heard. We could use the help. But you might want to go check up and down County Road 16, just to make sure you didn't overlook anything. We want to make sure we look like we know what we're doing around here."

Having ulterior motive, Lt Finch said, "Sure boss, I'm already one step ahead of you. I'm on my way."

With no time to waste, Lt. Finch quickly got to his squad car and sped out to see Mr. Tincher.

CHAPTER 12

While speeding up the long driveway, Lt. Finch started blowing his horn trying to get Mr. Tincher's attention. As he parked his car in front of the house, Mr. Tincher was outside waiting. He shouted, "What in the heck is with you and all the honking?!"

"We've got major problems coming our way." fretted Lt. Finch.

"Calm down. What are you talking about?"

"This place is fixin' to be flooded with law enforcement, from county deputies all the way up to possibly the Texas Rangers."

"Texas Rangers, huh. I've never had the privilege to meet a professional baseball player."

"You lug nut! I'm talking about the most respected law enforcement in Texas." fumed Lt. Finch.

Mr. Tincher laughed, "I'm just jerking your chain. I know who they are."

"I don't understand how you can be so relaxed. This is serious." warned Lt. Finch.

"What are they planning on doing?" Mr. Tincher

asked.

"My guess is, they'll search up and down this county road. If they find one shred of evidence that the Shannon brothers or Game Warden Jackson had been here, they won't stop searching. I'm sure they'll be bringing out the bloodhounds too. When they pick up a scent they can track it for miles. The only thing that might save us is, the weatherman said there's rain in the forecast for the next few days. Hopefully the bad weather will keep them away."

"I found the tracks the Game Warden left on my property. I have a plan to hide them."

"How are you going to do that?" questioned Lt. Finch.

Mr. Tincher pointed to his large herd of cattle.

"I'm simply going to feed my cows along the path of footprints that were left behind. With ninety head of cattle tromping along on this wet field, the only thing you're going to find is hoof prints."

Lt. Finch thought about it.

"That's a brilliant idea. But what about the prints in the ditch next to your fence?"

"I can saddle up my horse and take a ride over there. I'm sure I can take care of them too."

Feeling less anxious now, Lt. Finch got back into his patrol car.

"Sounds like you've got your side covered. I'll take care of the rest."

Leaving the farm, Lt. Finch felt more confident now than he did before.

CHAPTER 13

That afternoon, as predicted, numerous sheriff's deputy cars had arrived. They were parked all along the county road. The deputies wore their rain gear while they searched for clues out in the cold rain. After searching for hours and not finding anything, Sheriff Thomas John notified his deputies over the radio to end the search. As Lt. Finch slowly drove his squad car passed the slew of deputies, he stopped beside the sheriff's car. He rolled down his window.

"Any luck Sheriff?"

"No. It's raining too hard right now. The only thing we've found are horse tracks along the side of the road. When it ever quits raining we'll bring the bloodhounds out. But then again it may be too late to pick up a scent."

"Tell you what Sheriff. I'll be glad help out. I'm going to go up here and talk to Mr. Tincher and see if he's seen anything suspicious going on around here. If anything happened, he would be the first to know."

"Thanks for your help." replied Sheriff John.

Standing on his back porch looking through a pair

of binoculars, Mr. Tincher watched as the deputies got into their squad cars and started to disperse from the area. He then panned over and saw Lt. Finch pulling up his drive way. Letting the binoculars hang down by its leather strap from around his neck, Mr. Tincher then walked back into his house to meet Lt. Finch.

Standing on his front porch, he waved at Lt. Finch to come inside. Running from his car, he splashed muddy water all over his pants before reaching the shelter of the front porch.

"Come inside. Get out of the cold rain." insisted Mr. Tincher.

After wiping his shoes off, Lt. Finch carefully stepped inside the warm house. Mr. Tincher handed him a towel and impatiently asked, "So what did they say? Are they coming back?"

After drying his face, Lt. Finch laughed, "You old son of a gun. Covering those tracks like you did, worked. That was pure genius."

But then he cautioned, "It's not over with yet. When the rain is over, they'll be back. So, don't let your guard down. I'll keep you informed. I better be getting back to the station." Lt. Finch handed the towel back to Mr. Tincher, "Thanks for the use of your towel."

CHAPTER 14

After two days of constant raining, the sun finally made its appearance. Deputies Wes Sullins and Daniel Gates decided to take advantage of the break in the weather so they loaded up two bloodhound dogs to join in on the journey to County Road 16. Trying to find a dry place to park off the narrow road, the deputies chose the entrance to Mr. Tincher's property. As soon as the dogs were freed from their leashes, they put their noses to the ground and were on the move. The continuous baying from the dogs and the shouting of encouragement from the deputies, quickly got Mr. Tincher's attention. Grabbing his rifle and binoculars, he kept a close eye on them from his back porch.

After searching for two hours without any scent to be found, Deputy Gates radioed in to Lt. Greg Zahirniak, at the sheriff's office.

"Deputy Gates to Lt. Zahirniak."

"Go ahead with your traffic deputy."

"Sir, we've been out here on County Road 16 for

the past two hours and the dogs haven't picked up on anything. Please advise on what you want us to do."

"10-4 on your last transmission. Go ahead and load up and come on back in."

"10-4" Deputy Gates responded.

Watching the deputies leave with the two bloodhounds gave Mr. Tincher a feeling of relief.

Back at the Willow Springs Police Department, Sheila Ridgeway, an investigative news reporter from Dallas and her camera man, Jace Montgomery entered the station. Standing in the lobby with her microphone in her hand, she patted her hair and asked, "How do I look?"

Looking through the camera, Mr. Montgomery responded, "You look great."

"Thanks. Now, let's see if we can find who's in charge around here." As Ms. Ridgeway began to walk down the corridor, she was stopped by Ms. Speaker.

"Sorry ma'am. You're not allowed down here unless you're being escorted. How can I help you?"

"I'm Sheila Ridgeway investigative reporter from Dallas. This is Jace Montgomery, my camera man. Can I talk to whoever is in charge?"

"That would be Chief McKechnie. Let me check with him first."

Ms. Speaker walked to Chief McKechnie's office. She knocked on the door.

"Yes." he answered.

Ms. Speaker opened the door and quietly said, "Sir, we have a news reporter here. She wishes to speak with you."

He let out a sigh, "Sure, send her in."

Ms. Speaker looked back down the corridor and motioned for them to come down. Entering Chief

McKechnie's office, Ms. Ridgeway produced her press credentials.

"Chief McKechnie, I'm Sheila Ridgeway an investigative reporter with KCTV out of Dallas. I was wanting to know if I could get an exclusive interview with you about the disappearance of the Shannon brothers."

"We've had to add one more to the list of people we are searching for."

"Oh my." she said with a grimaced look.

"Game Warden Jess Jackson, disappeared a few days ago. No one has heard from him either."

"Do you think there's any connections?"

"Not for sure. We haven't found any evidence to make that decision yet. But we're digging."

"Can you tell me more?"

"No ma'am. The investigations are still on going in all three cases. But if anyone out there in the public eye has any information, we would appreciate any tip that you can give."

"Thank you Chief, for the short interview. Hope it helps you in finding these individuals."

While Ms. Ridgeway and Mr. Montgomery were walking to their van, they overheard two police officers talking about the disappearances.

"Hey Jones, have they found anything over on County Road 16?"

"I don't think so. There's been a lot of searching going on. I believe there's a connection somewhere with that county road and the disappearances."

Sitting in the van, Ms. Ridgeway looked at Mr. Montgomery. "Did you hear that?" she whispered.

"I did, so what."

She beamed, "Do you know what this means. If I

crack this case before the police can, I'll surely get my promotion to news anchor." She started clapping her hands together unable to contain her excitement. "Heck, I might even win a Peabody Award."

"Yeah or get yourself in trouble for obstructing an ongoing investigation." he warned.

"Oh come on. Don't be a party pooper."

"What do you propose we do now?" he asked.

"We need to find this County Road 16, that's what I'm proposing."

While exiting the parking lot on to Main street, Mr. Montgomery realized he needed to fill up his gas tank.

"Ms. Ridgeway, I need to find a gas station. If we're going to be searching all over the county, we don't need to run out, on some godforsaken back road."

"You're right. I need to find a lady's room too."

While traveling down Main Street, Ms. Ridgeway spotted and then pointed to Leo's One Stop.

"Pull in there. Maybe someone inside can tell me where this county road is located."

After filling the gas tank, Mr. Montgomery waited inside the van. Moments later, Ms. Ridgeway left the establishment tight-lipped and walking as fast as she could. "Any luck in getting directions?"

After exhaling she said, "Take a right at the stop sign. County Road 16 is five miles out."

"What's wrong?"

"That has to be the dirtiest restroom ever."

Mr. Montgomery started laughing as they departed Leo's.

CHAPTER 15

After placing orders all morning for his side business, Lt. Finch decided to stop for lunch before picking up his merchandise from Mr. Tincher. Walking into Mabel's Café, he saw Chief McKechnie sitting at a booth by himself.

"Hey, Chief. You mind if I join you?"

"Not at all. Have a seat."

While Lt. Finch is looking through the menu, Chief McKechnie asks, "What have you been up to today?"

"Not much. Just trying to enjoy the day off."

Chief McKechnie noticed Finch was wearing a rather expensive wrist watch. Not to pry into one's business, he refrained from even complimenting him on his taste.

Waitress Cari Barnes, a twenty-eight-year-old bomb shell, stopped by the booth.

"Hey Sugar, what will it be today?" she asked in her usual flirtatious voice.

"You know, what I always get. But I need it to-go

this time.

"So, you want your burger and fries dropped in a sack huh?"

"Yeah, I don't have time to visit today. I have some errands to run."

"Sure Sweetie, we'll get it on the grill."

Chief McKechnie winked at him as she left.

"Boy I think she's hot for you. Mama better not find out."

What the chief didn't know is that Cari is one of Lt. Finch's customers.

"Awe, she doesn't mean nothing by it. I think she's wanting someone to replace her old man. He's doing time in the state prison."

"Hey Finch, I had a news reporter stop in this morning. We did a short interview. I hope someone out there can give us a hand in solving these cases."

"Boss, was it necessary? We already have enough people investigating these cases. We don't need any interlopers interfering with us."

"I think it will help. Someone from the outside may see something that we're overlooking." Chief McKechnie pointed out.

Cari walked up and set a sack on the table.

"Here's your lunch Sugar."

Lt. Finch handed her a twenty-dollar bill.

"Keep the change."

"Wow, thanks big spender."

"See ya Chief. I've got something to do."

Looking through the window blinds at Lt. Finch getting into his new car, Chief McKechnie became a little suspicious. He wondered how he can afford a nice sports car and an extravagant watch on an eighteen thousand dollar a year salary.

CHAPTER 16

While Mr. Montgomery drove the van, Ms. Ridgeway kept on the lookout for County Road 16.

"How far have we gone?" Ms. Ridgeway asked.

Looking at the odometer, he answered back, "We've gone close to five miles. We should be getting close."

Just as they passed over a hill, Ms. Ridgeway sees a road on the right.

"Slow down. These road signs are hard to read."

The numbers on the small green sign were faded.

Mr. Montgomery slowly entered the road and stopped. Ms. Ridgeway got out of the van so she could get a closer look at the sign.

She yelled, "This is it Montgomery! We found it."

Quickly returning to the van, she said, "Now, let's see if this old road has any secrets it wants to divulge."

After driving a half of a mile down the old secluded road, they came upon the tunnel of trees.

"Oh my." Ms. Ridgeway gasped. "I can only

imagine how scary this place is when the foliage is out."

Feeling scared, she reached behind her to lock the door.

Mr. Montgomery laughed, "There's nothing to be scared of. It's still daylight."

"Don't you stop this van until we reach the other side. And please drive a little faster too."

Once they had reached the end of the thick tree line, Ms. Ridgeway felt at ease.

"Ok, so what do we do now?" queried Mr. Montgomery.

"Keep driving. Maybe we can find someone who lives around here that would be willing to talk to us."

As they approached Mr. Tincher's driveway, they stopped. The gate to his driveway was closed. Mr. Montgomery grabbed his camera. While he looked through it, he zoomed in on Mr. Tincher's house using a high powered telephoto lens.

"I guess we need to keep going. There's a pickup parked in front of the house, but I don't see anyone moving about the place."

"Let's go Mr. Montgomery. Let's see what else we can find."

As they continued on their path into deeper seclusion, Lt. Finch arrived at Mr. Tincher's house.

As customary, he let his presence be known by honking his horn.

Mr. Tincher yelled from the barn.

"I'll be right there!" After closing the barn door, he tried to wipe the dust from his overalls.

"Feeding old Killer, his corn can be a messy job."
"Frank, I need to make some deliveries this afternoon. Has Ross got any bagged up and ready to

go?"

"Yeah, I have some in the house. How much you need?"

"I need around ten kilos."

"Wow!" blurted Mr. Tincher.

"Hey everyone likes Willow Springs finest."

"Come on in the house. Let's get you fixed up."

After reaching the end of the county road, Mr. Montgomery stopped at an intersection.

"Ok. Where do we go now?" he asked.

Feeling dejected for not finding anything but farm land along the road, she suggested, "We better go back the way we came. One wrong turn and we'll be lost for sure."

As they passed back by Mr. Tincher's driveway, Ms. Ridgeway notice that the gate was open.

"Stop!" she demanded.

"I guess you want me to drive up to a total stranger's house, without being invited."

"Please." she begged.

Unwillingly, he slowly pulled into the driveway. Mr. Montgomery felt uneasy after passing a 'NO TRESPASSING' sign that clearly had bullet holes in it. If the holes there were meant to intimidate, it clearly worked. Being cautious, he continued driving up the long and winding driveway.

As they got closer to the house, they saw Lt. Finch quickly toss a tightly wrapped plastic black bag into the trunk of his car. Mr. Tincher confronted them before they could get out and introduce themselves. "What are ya'll doing out here?!" snapped Mr. Tincher

"This is private property. Didn't you see the dadgum 'NO TRESPASSING' sign?!"

Feeling nervous, Ms. Ridgeway said in a low tone, "Sir please calm down. All I wanted, was to ask you a few questions about the disappearance's in Willow Springs."

Mr. Tincher began to lose his patients, "I don't have a clue about anyone missing." He then pointed to his driveway, "You need to leave my property NOW!"

"Yes sir." babbled Mr. Montgomery.

Scared, he hastily put the van in reverse and they quickly sped away.

Feeling ticked off, Ms. Ridgeway fumed, "Man what a jerk! There's no reason for him to talk to us that way."

Mr. Montgomery pointed out, "Did you notice how the old man immediately tried to distract us from seeing what was tossed into the car?"

"Yeah, he did seem overly anxious. I wonder why?"

"There's no reason to get all worked up over a black plastic bag."

"It depends on what's in it." Mr. Montgomery hinted.

Being sarcastic, she asked, "Ok Sherlock, what are you suggesting?"

"The way the bag was taped up like a brick, that's how drug smugglers transport their drugs."

"Really. I know it's just speculation, but I wonder if it would be worth dropping an anonymous note to Chief McKechnie. If nothing else than to make the old man mad."

"I tell you what we can do. We'll park at the end of the road." Mr. Montgomery then grabbed a road map from his dashboard. "I'll pretend I'm looking at the map, as soon as the Camaro passes by, I'll take a picture of it. You can send it in with your note."

"Sounds great." she said with a devilish grin.

CHAPTER 17

Three days had passed since Chief McKechnie's interview with Ms. Ridgeway. With no new leads in the cases, he felt pressured into doing something. Taking a break from reading the mail, he called Major Dan Johnson of the Texas Rangers.

"Hello, this is Major Johnson."

"Major Johnson, this is Chief McKechnie with the Willow Springs Police Department. Can I have just a moment of your time?"

"Sure Chief, what can I help you with?"

"I've have three missing person cases that I need some help with."

"Sure, I can help. I'll have one of my field lieutenants to contact you."

"Thank you, sir."

After making the call, he felt some sort of relief. He then continued to browse through the mail. One letter in particular caught his attention. It didn't have a return address. After opening the envelope, he pulled out a letter along with two pictures. The letter was not signed. It read, '*I think this man is dealing drugs.*'

In the first picture he recognized the house belonging to Frank Tincher. The second picture was of the back end of Chevy Camaro. It didn't look familiar but he was able to make out the license plate. He placed the letter and picture inside his desk drawer. He didn't give it too much credence since the note wasn't signed and the envelope didn't have a return address.

Before he left his office for lunch, Chief McKechnie got a phone call.

"Hello, Chief McKechnie speaking."

"Good afternoon Chief, this is Lt. Toney Carrizales of the Texas Rangers. My supervisor asked me to call you."

"Yes sir, I would like to set up a meeting with you. Could we meet tomorrow for lunch?"

"Yes of course. Where would you like to meet?"

"I don't want to meet here in Willow Springs. Are you familiar with the town of Arden? It's our neighboring town to the east."

"Yes sir, I know right were Arden is located."

"Let's meet at the little Mexican restaurant that's downtown called, Hector's. I'll meet you there at twelve sharp. I'll be in plain clothes."

CHAPTER 18

After pouring herself a cup of coffee, Ms. Speaker looked at the clock on the wall. It showed to be eight a.m. She began to wonder why Chief McKechnie hadn't made it in yet. He's always at the police station by seven-thirty a.m.

Before she got started filing yesterday's police reports, her phone rang.

She answered, "Willow Springs Police Department."

"Ms. Speaker, Chief here. I'm going to take the day off. I've got some things I need to do. I'll check in periodically, to see how things are going. Have Lt. Finch to take charge for me."

"Sure thing, boss."

Later that morning, at eleven-forty-five, Chief McKechnie is sitting in a booth at the back of Hector's restaurant. While he was busy reading a newspaper, he hears a man's voice.

"Sir, are you Mr. McKechnie?"

Putting his newspaper down, he saw a tall, slender built gentleman wearing a white cowboy hat.

Chief McKechnie stood up and shook hands with the stranger.

"Yes, I'm Chief McKechnie."

"Hello sir, I'm Lt. Tony Carrizales. I'm with the Texas Rangers."

"Have a seat Mr. Carrizales. It's a pleasure to meet you."

Once they were seated, a waitress handed them their menu's.

"What will you gentleman like to drink?"

"I believe I'll have a glass of tea." said Mr. Carrizales.

"I'll have the same." responded Chief McKechnie.

After the waitress had departed, Mr. Carrizales asked, "How can I help?"

"I need some help investigating these disappearances in my town."

Chief McKechnie handed Mr. Carrizales the letter he'd received the previous day.

"I'm a little concerned with what's inside."

Mr. Carrizales read the note and looked at the two photos.

"Who's house?"

"The house belongs to Frank Tincher. He's an old farmer that's been in the community all of his life. He's never been a problem. He pretty much stays to himself."

"What about the car?"

"I ran the plates and they belong to Chris Finch." He then let out a sigh, "He's my lieutenant."

"Has he given you any reason to think he's dirty?"

"He's a good officer, but I think he's developed a gambling problem. He likes to go to the casinos a couple times a month. He drives a new sportscar and

I saw him wearing a new Rolex watch. I can't figure out how he can do all of this, on an eighteen-thousand-dollar salary."

"Is it possible he could have won the watch or been giving to him as a gift from a family member?"

"I don't think so. I've heard him talk about the struggles his family has had over the years. One more thing that raised an alarm. He got irritated when I told him that I was going to ask the Texas Rangers for help. He didn't think we needed any outside help. He's been doing the investigation himself."

"You want me to follow him?" asked Mr. Carrizales.

"Yes. I want someone that's not from this area. I feel bad about having one of my own employees tailed."

"Chief, don't feel bad. Maybe there's nothing to this. I'll follow him for a couple of weeks and then report back to you."

"Thanks Mr. Carrizales. That would be greatly appreciated."

After agreeing on their plan, the waitress arrived with their drinks and asked, "You gentlemen ready to order?"

CHAPTER 19

Later that same afternoon, Travis Smith, owner of Smith's Land Surveying Company, entered the police department.

"Hello Ms. Speaker, is the Chief in. I would like to talk to him if he has the time."

"Hey Travis, Chief McKechnie is out of the office today. He left Lt. Finch in charge. I'm sure he can help you."

Hearing their conversation, Lt. Finch stepped outside of his office.

"Hello Travis, come on in to my office and have a seat."

They shook hands as Travis entered in. Closing the door behind him, Lt. Finch asked, "What brings you in here this afternoon?"

"Lt. Finch, there may be nothing to this, but today while I was surveying old man Buford Callahan's property, I saw something that I thought I should bring to your attention."

Knowing that Mr. Callahan's property is next to

Mr. Tincher, he curiously asked, "What is it?"

"While I was surveying sections of Mr. Callahan's land, I smelled a terrible odor coming from Mr. Tincher's property."

"Awe, it's probably an old cow that died."

"I looked in the woods where the buzzards were circling above, the only thing I found was some greenhouses. There must have been ten to twelve of 'em."

"So, Mr. Tincher has greenhouses; what's the big deal about that?"

"I've never seen a greenhouse with a portable diesel generator before."

"Maybe he's trying to compete in the nursery business."

"There's only one nursery business in this town and that's Charles Swanson. He doesn't even use diesel generators. I wonder if there could be some nefarious activities going on." Travis pondered.

"I wouldn't worry about that. Mr. Tincher has been around for a long time. He's never been in any kind of trouble. By the way, you said you were surveying sections of Mr. Callahan's property. What's he plan on doing?"

"He's sectioning up the land for development."

Lt. Finch thought to himself, *"That's just great, there goes our privacy."*

"Thanks Travis, I'll pass the information on to the Chief."

CHAPTER 20

After two weeks of reconnaissance, Ranger Carrizales called Chief McKechnie to report his findings.

"Hello, Chief McKechnie speaking."

"Good morning Chief, this is Ranger Carrizales. I wanted to touch base with you and to give you a completed report on my two-week surveillance of Lt. Finch."

"Sure. Did you find out anything?"

"I'm afraid the drop note you received is credible."

Chief McKechnie leaned back in his chair and exhaled loudly.

Feeling disgusted he said, "I was afraid of that. Guess we need to plan our next course of action."

"Hey Chief, let's meet tomorrow at our little restaurant in Arden. I have some photos for you to look at."

"That's fine. I'll have Sheriff John to join us. I'll see you tomorrow, twelve sharp."

~~~

After placing their orders for lunch, Ranger Carrizales reached into his coat pocket and produced an envelope which contained numerous photographs that were taken over the two-week surveillance period. He made comments on them as he passed them out, one at a time.

Scanning through the photos, Chief McKechnie shook his head, "There's no way Lt. Finch can explain his way out of this."

Mr. Carrizales commented, "He's a busy man on his days off. He makes his deliveries to Sally's Flower Shop when there's no customers around. Leo's One Stop gets theirs after they're closed. The residential customers get theirs on Friday night."

"Mr. Carrizales, you sure did your homework." praised Sheriff John.

"Check this out." Mr. Carrizales added. "My informant told me if you wanted to purchase marijuana from one of these establishments, you had to call it by its name. He tried to purchase some from Sally's and they got offended by him for insinuating that they deal drugs. He went in the following week and ask for some 'Willow Spring' and was able to make a purchase."

"Ok, so what's our game plan on making these busts?" questioned Chief McKechnie.

"My suggestion is to wait until next week when everyone makes their purchase, then we bust everyone at the same time."

"Sounds good Mr. Carrizales. It's going to take a lot of manpower and precise coordinating." remarked Chief McKechnie.

"We got a week to get everything planned, sir."

CHAPTER 21

Six a.m. couldn't come quick enough for Chief McKechnie. Another sleepless night thinking about the betrayal of the badge by his friend and co-worker, started to take its toll on him. Last night was especially rough, knowing in two days he would be arresting one of his very own. After getting dressed, his wife Marsha asked, "What would you like for breakfast?"

"Honey, I'll pick something up later." he yawned. "I don't have an appetite this morning."

"What's wrong Tom? You've haven't been acting like yourself the past few days."

"It's nothing for you to worry about. I'm sure things will get better soon."

While driving to work, Chief McKechnie knew he needed to perk up. If he showed any signs that he was upset or disappointed in Lt. Finch, it could raise a red flag and cause a disruption in the upcoming raid.

"Good morning Chief." greeted Ms. Speaker as she poured herself a cup of coffee.

"Good morning Ms. Speaker."

"Boss, the coffee is fresh. Would you like a cup?"

"Yes, please."

After filling up his cup, he stopped by Lt. Finch's office.

"Got any new leads on the three missing persons?"

"Nothing to speak of Chief. I'm hoping someone will come forth with some new information."

"Just stay on top of it."

Chief McKechnie knew he didn't want to say too much, but he wanted to let Finch know they would never stop looking. "If there's any criminal activity involved in these disappearance's, someone will eventually slip-up, and when they do, we're gonna get 'em."

After Chief McKechnie departed, Lt. Finch grinned, and let out a small chuckle. He thought, *'As long as you have the fox guarding the hen house, you'll never solve these cases.'*

After spending the morning organizing his files, Lt. Finch's stomach started to growl. He knew it had to be getting close to lunch time. He looked at his watch and it was confirmed. It was twelve o'clock. Tending to his hunger pain was top priority now. Leaving the rest of the files on his desk to be filed after lunch, he left his office. As he passed by Chief McKechnie's office he stopped and asked, "Hey Chief, I'm going to get a bite to eat. You want to join me?"

"No thank you. I'm waiting for a phone call. Thanks' anyway."

While Chief McKechnie was waiting for a phone call from Ranger Carrizales, he received a call from

Travis Smith.

"Hello, Chief McKechnie speaking."

"Hello Chief, this is Travis Smith. How are you doing today?"

"Hello Travis, I'm fine. How's the business?"

"Busy sir. Hey, the reason why I called; did you get the information that I gave to Lt. Finch? He was supposed to pass it on to you."

Chief McKechnie frowned, "No, he hasn't said a word to me. What did you need to tell me?"

"Chief, I think you need to check out Frank Tincher's farm. While I was surveying Mr. Callahan's property, I smelt the god awfulness smell coming from Tincher's property. The smell was coming from the greenhouse's that he has hidden in the woods."

Chief McKechnie leaned back in his chair.

"Well, well. You say he has some greenhouse's huh?"

"Yes, at least ten to twelve of them. They even have their own portable diesel generators."

"Wow that's interesting. Sounds like he has an expensive setup. The last time I was out at Mr. Swanson's nursery he didn't have that nice of one."

"Chief, Mr. Swanson is the only nursery business around. I know I should mind my own business, but why would Mr. Tincher need something so extravagant?"

Chief didn't answer. He thought, now everything is falling into place now. Lt. Finch's new sports car, the Rolex watch, the trips to the casino's and not wanting outside help in the investigations.

"Chief you still there?"

"I'm sorry. I got to thinking about something. I wouldn't worry about Mr. Tincher. We can't investigate without probable cause. But thank you for your information."

After talking to Mr. Smith, Chief McKechnie called Ranger Carrizales.

"This is Lt. Carrizales with the Texas Rangers."

"Lt. Carrizales, this is Chief McKechnie. I just received some information that I think you might find interesting."

"Good. Let's have it."

"I just heard Mr. Tincher has at least twelve greenhouses hidden in the woods on his property. Each has its own generator to supply electricity."

"Hum. Sounds like Mr. Tincher could be in the marijuana business."

"That's what I am thinking."

"Chief, we have the plan all worked out for the raid. Sheriff John is going to supply us with some of his deputies. I have some State Troopers that are involved in the drug task force that are going to lend a hand. Are your officers still unaware about what's fixing to transpire?"

"My men know nothing."

"Good. I'll see you in a couple of days."

After lunch, Lt. Finch returned back to work. Before he could make it to his office, Chief McKechnie asked him to step inside his office.

"Hey Finch, I wanted to thank you for covering for me the other day."

"Sure. No problem Chief."

"It's nice to know I have someone capable of running the department when I'm not around. Did I receive any messages that needed my attention?"

"No sir. Not one."

"Thank you, Finch. You can carry on."

"Hey boss, before I go, you mind if I take off early this afternoon. I'd like to start my days off early."

"Not at all. You can go now if you'd like."

"Thanks."

While Lt. Finch walked away, Chief McKechnie realized, that was going to be the last time he seen Chris Finch as a free man.

CHAPTER 22

Bright and early the following morning, Lt. Finch was already out and about making his rounds taking orders. Once he was done, he couldn't wait to see Mr. Tincher. He just placed his biggest order yet. Feeling excited about the amount of money he was about to make, he eagerly sped out of town to meet his supplier.

Parked in front of Mr. Tincher's house, Lt. Finch, as always, gave two courteous bursts on the horn. After looking through the window blinds and seeing it was Lt. Finch, Mr. Tincher walked out onto his front porch.

"Good news!" Finch shouted. "I just sold the largest amount of Willow Spring today."

Mr. Tincher grinned, "How much young man?"

"I sold twenty-five kilos' today. That's nearly forty-four thousand dollars. I hope you have it ready."

"I should. Ross has been busy chopping and baggin'."

After loading his car with the valuable

merchandise, Lt. Finch hit the road with dollar signs in his sights.

~~~

Once the deliveries were made, Lt. Finch was carrying more money than he had ever seen before. His cut in the business was twenty percent. Lt. Finch figured he would make close to nine thousand dollars. Not bad for a day's work. It didn't take long before he started dreaming about all the different ways he would spend the money if it were all his. Greed, one of the seven deadly sins overcame him.

Before he had reached Mr. Tincher's house, Lt. Finch had stuffed several handfuls of bills underneath his car seat thinking the old farmer wouldn't miss it.

As he slowly approached Mr. Tincher's house, he could see him sitting on his porch.

"Welcome home Finch. I hope you brought plenty of moolah back with you."

Lt. Finch grabbed the laundry bags full of cash and followed Mr. Tincher into the house.

Mr. Tincher opened the refrigerator door, "Finch you want a beer?"

"Sure."

Lt. Finch opened the laundry bags and poured the money on the kitchen table. Mr. Tincher handed him a bottle of beer.

"Look at all of that money. I'm glad we don't have to count it. It would take all day."

"What are you talking about?"

Mr. Tincher went to his bed room and brought back an electronic currency counter.

Lt. Finch became frightened. He knew what it was.

He remembered seeing them at the casinos. Lt. Finch started to feel nervous because how would he explain the missing cash.

Mr. Tincher placed a small stack of bills into the machine. Once the machine was turned on, the money was counted in a matter seconds. Lt. Finch stared nervously at the currency counter, hoping Mr. Tincher's own calculations were off a few thousand dollars.

Once the machine had completed its job, Mr. Tincher compared his own figures to the digital readout on the machine. He shook his head and rubbed his scruffy beard.

"Looks like we're short close to three thousand dollars."

Lt. Finch stammered, "Maybe the machine miscounted."

Mr. Tincher looked at Lt Finch and winked, "You sure you're not skimming off the top?"

Sounding offended, Finch answered, "Of course not."

"Hey Ross! Come in here." hollered Mr. Tincher

As Ross entered the kitchen Mr. Tincher asked, "Then you wouldn't have any objections if ole Ross here searched through your car."

Nervous as he was, Lt. Finch tried to remain calm. He knew the situation that he was in could become volatile at any moment.

"Sure, go ahead."

Ten minutes later, Ross returned cradling both arms full of cash.

"Where did you find it Ross?"

"It was hidden underneath his seat."

"What am I going to do with you Finch? I can't

have you working with me and not be able to trust you."

"Tell you what. Pay me a hundred thousand dollars, then I'll leave the business and keep our little secrets."

"And what if I don't, what are you going to do?"

"I'll arrest you for murder and drug charges."

Mr. Tincher laughed. He then pulled a revolver from a cabinet drawer and pointed it at Finch.

"You're in no position to make a deal."

"Hey, what are you doing! Don't shoot!" pleaded Finch. "Forget what I said. Keep the money. I won't say a word."

"I know you won't say a word."

Mr. Tincher pulled the trigger, shooting Finch in the head, killing him instantly.

CHAPTER 23

Four-thirty in the afternoon, Chief McKechnie is sitting at his desk. He felt anxious all day thinking about what was about to transpire. He prayed that all went well and that no one got hurt. He received a phone call from Ranger Carrizales.

"Hello, Chief McKechnie speaking."

"Good afternoon Chief, Ranger Carrizales speaking. We're all set to meet at the staging area six-thirty sharp."

"Good. I'll see you then."

As he was preparing to leave for the day, Sheila Ridgeway and Jace Montgomery entered the police station.

"Hello Chief, you remember me?"

He thought, *'Oh man I ain't got time for this.'*

He smiled and said, "I'm sorry, I don't have time right now to give you an interview."

"Chief, did you get the letter I mailed to you?"

He thought for a moment, "No, I don't recall getting a letter from you."

"I sent it anonymously. It had a photo of a Chevy

Camaro."

"You sent that?"

"Yes, I did. Did it stir up any interest?"

"Oh boy. Did it ever."

"Can you give us the status on the investigation?"

"I can't tell you the status because I don't want to hinder all the work that's been involved."

Ms. Ridgeway frowned, "You can't tell me nothing, huh?"

Chief McKechnie looked around the room before he spoke. He lowered his voice and said, "Do you want to have the biggest scoop of your career?"

Ms. Ridgeway's eyes lit up.

"Since you were the source that got the ball rolling in this investigation, be at Mr. Tincher's farm at eight p.m. tonight. Not a minute earlier."

The staging area for the raids was located in an old abandoned cotton gin on the outskirts of Willow Springs. Chief McKechnie, Sheriff John and Ranger Carrizales and the members of the strike force team were gathered together finalizing their plan of action. After issuing each team member an assigned target to be raided, Ranger Carrizales looked at his watch and said, "Ok men, lets synchronize our watches. My watch is showing six-thirty-two. At seven o'clock sharp, we hit 'em quick."

After everyone had set their watches, Ranger Carrizales wished them good luck.

Chief McKechnie and six members of the strike force were assigned to serve a search warrant on Mr. Frank Tincher's property.

After feeding Killer, Mr. Tincher and Ross were finished working for the day. As Mr. Tincher walked from the barn, he saw two cars turn off their headlights while slowly driving up his driveway. Mr. Tincher quickly ran back into the barn.

"Get back Ross!" Looking through a small gap in the wall of the barn, he saw the two cars park in front of his house. Being unmarked cars, Mr. Tincher didn't have a clue who they were. As the team assembled, Mr. Tincher heard Chief McKechnie giving directions to where the greenhouses were located. As the team scattered about, Chief McKechnie knocked on Mr. Tincher's front door.

"Police! Open up! We have a search warrant!"

Mr. Tincher pointed to the back of the barn.

"Ross get out of here. Use that back door."

After knocking numerous times without getting a response, he decided to walk around to the back of the house. As he stepped off the front porch, Chief McKechnie heard the sound of a squeaking door closing, coming from the barn. He decided to investigate the noise. The closer he got to the barn, Chief McKechnie repeated, "Police! I have a search warrant Mr. Tincher!"

Before he entered the barn, Chief McKechnie took a deep breath and then retrieved his service revolver from his holster. As he carefully walked through the barn, wherever he aimed his flashlight, his gun was pointed in the same spot. The sound of field rats squeaking and scurrying across the support beams in the barn made his skin crawl.

It wasn't long before his attention was drawn to three large objects, each one covered by a large tarp. Slowly trying to walk through the maze of farm equipment that lay in his path, he got close enough that he could see that they were vehicles. Chief McKechnie using the hand that held his gun, raised one of the tarps just high enough where he could see the Texas Game Warden decal on the pickup door. He then lifted the tarp on the next vehicle. It was the Ford pickup belonging to the Shannon brothers. The third vehicle caught him by surprise. It was the Camaro belonging to Lt. Finch. He had an eerie feeling about the welfare of these individuals.

As he began to make his way back to the front of the barn, the large door opened. Standing in the doorway was Mr. Tincher and his six-hundred-pound companion.

"Mr. Tincher, I have a search warrant. We need to talk."

"I don't like people coming on my property uninvited. You know what I do when I catch them."

Mr. Tincher patted Killer on the back and said, "Sick'em boy!"

As soon as Killer took off running towards Chief McKechnie, Mr. Tincher closed the door locking the two inside. Chief McKechnie, pointed his gun and fired three rounds at the beast, but to no avail, he kept charging, Chief McKechnie knew he had to get out of the reach of this powerful animal. He aimed his flashlight to his left side and saw a tall stack of hay. While he tried to climb to safety, the hog rammed his body into the stack of hay, causing Chief McKechnie and the hay to come tumbling down. Pinned down underneath the hay Chief McKechnie lost his gun and flashlight. Killer kept rooting away the bales of hay trying to get at Chief McKechnie. Thankfully one of his team members, Officer Knowles, heard the three gunshots from Chief McKechnie. To gain entry, Officer Knowles had to shoot the padlock off the barn door. Not a moment to spare, Officer Knowles ran in and found the hog. With one last bale separating Chief McKechnie and his gruesome demise, Officer Knowles aimed in and shot the hog ending his thirst for killing.

"Chief are you Ok?"

Trying to catch his breath, "Yeah. I'll be fine. Thanks for saving my life."

"It's a good thing I stayed close, or you might have been in real trouble."

"Hey we need to find Mr. Tincher. We can't let him get away."

Officer Knowles radioed for backup.

"We need assistance in the barn. The suspect has gotten away!"

Mr. Tincher tried to flee the scene by stealing one of the unmarked cars, but he was blocked from leaving by no other than the KCTV news van driven by Mr. Montgomery. Before Mr. Tincher could flee on foot, the rest of the strike force team members had him surrounded with their gun drawn on him.

As Chief McKechnie and officer Knowles exited the barn, they saw Mr. Tincher face down on the ground, with his hands cuffed behind him. Standing over him Officer Austin said, "If it wasn't for the three warning shots, he may have gotten away."

Chief McKechnie looked at Officer Knowles and grinned.

"Warning shots. Really?"

Officer Davis handed Chief McKechnie a badge and said, "Sir we found this in one the greenhouses in the woods."

Wiping the dirt from it, Chief McKechnie knew it belong to Lt. Finch.

"He's dead?"

"Sir, we've found what we believe to be four shallow graves. One of them looks like it was freshly dug."

As they placed Mr. Tincher in the backseat of one of the unmarked cars, Ms. Ridgeway and her camera man Mr. Montgomery were setting up to go live on the air. One of the members of the strike force team ordered them to leave.

"Ma'am you need to get back. We don't have time for this right now."

Ms. Ridgeway looked at Chief McKechnie.

"I thought we had a deal."

"Officer, I'll talk to her. I owe it to her."

After giving Ms. Ridgeway the scoop of a lifetime, it was time to take Mr. Tincher to jail. As they traveled through the eerie tunnel of trees on County Road 16, Chief McKechnie looked at Mr. Tincher in his rear-view mirror and said, "Tincher, your drug business and murdering days are over with."

Staring out the side window, knowing this would be the last time he would get to see his home place again, Mr. Tincher saw his nephew Ross standing in the shadows holding and stroking a small pig. He looked back at Chief McKechnie with a grin and said, "I don't know about that Chief."

The End

ABOUT THE AUTHOR

David holds a degree in Applied Arts and Sciences from The University of Texas at Tyler.

He enjoys living the simple country life that East Texas has to offer.

David's been married for twenty-three years and has two daughters.

Made in the USA
Coppell, TX
13 December 2019

12874256R00046